Dear Parents:

Congratulations! Your child is taking the first steps on an exciting journey. The destination? Independent reading!

STEP INTO READING® will help your child get there. The program offers five steps to reading success. Each step includes fun stories and colorful art or photographs. In addition to original fiction and books with favorite characters, there are Step into Reading Non-Fiction Readers, Phonics Readers and Boxed Sets, Sticker Readers, and Comic Readers—a complete literacy program with something to interest every child.

Learning to Read, Step by Step!

Ready to Read   Preschool–Kindergarten
• big type and easy words • rhyme and rhythm • picture clues
For children who know the alphabet and are eager to begin reading.

Reading with Help   Preschool–Grade 1
• basic vocabulary • short sentences • simple stories
For children who recognize familiar words and sound out new words with help.

Reading on Your Own   Grades 1–3
• engaging characters • easy-to-follow plots • popular topics
For children who are ready to read on their own.

Reading Paragraphs   Grades 2–3
• challenging vocabulary • short paragraphs • exciting stories
For newly independent readers who read simple sentences with confidence.

Ready for Chapters   Grades 2–4
• chapters • longer paragraphs • full-color art
For children who want to take the plunge into chapter books but still like colorful pictures.

STEP INTO READING® is designed to give every child a successful reading experience. The grade levels are only guides; children will progress through the steps at their own speed, developing confidence in their reading.

Remember, a lifetime love of reading starts with a single step!

For Sofia
—N.E.

Special thanks to Kelsey Howard,
Sherin Kwan, and Alex Wiltshire

All rights reserved. Published in the United States by Random House Children's Books, a division of Penguin Random House LLC, 1745 Broadway, New York, NY 10019, and in Canada by Penguin Random House Canada Limited, Toronto.

Step into Reading, Random House, and the Random House colophon are registered trademarks of Penguin Random House LLC.

Visit us on the Web!
StepIntoReading.com
rhcbooks.com
minecraft.net
Educators and librarians, for a variety of teaching tools, visit us at RHTeachersLibrarians.com

ISBN 978-0-5934-3067-5 (trade)—ISBN 978-0-5934-3068-2 (lib. bdg.)—
ISBN 978-0-5934-3069-9 (ebook)

Printed in the United States of America
10 9 8 7 6 5 4 3 2

MINECRAFT

ESCAPE FROM THE NETHER!

by Nick Eliopulos

illustrated by Alan Batson

Random House 🏠 New York

4

Emmy and Birch
were ready for adventure!
Emmy had a brand-new helmet
and matching boots
made of yellow gold.
Birch had a brand-new sword
made of iron.

Byte, their loyal wolf,
just wanted to play.
"We can play fetch,"
said Emmy.
"Ready, boy?"
asked Birch.

"FETCH!"

7

Byte ran after the stick.
But he did not return.
"Where did he go?"
asked Birch.
They both called him.

They did not find Byte,
but they saw something
strange.
Beneath the trees,
they found
a rectangle of blocks
made of black obsidian.
The air glowed purple
inside it.

"It's a portal
to the Nether,"
said Emmy.
She put her hand
into the purple light.
Her hand disappeared!

"Do you think Byte
went through the portal?"
asked Birch.
"There is only one way
to find out," said Emmy.
"Come on!"

The two friends
leaped into the portal.
At first, Birch thought
they were still in the forest.

Then he saw that
the trees were
blue-green.
So was the grass.

Birch and Emmy climbed
a pair of vines
to get a better view
of the Nether.
Birch gasped in surprise.

He saw a gray desert.

He saw a red woodland.

And he saw an ocean of lava.

Birch had never seen any place
like this in Minecraft.
"Even the mushrooms are strange!"
Emmy told him with a laugh.
She put two blue-green fungi
in her inventory.

Setting out to find Byte,
they started walking.
The strange blue-green forest
became a strange red forest.

Birch raised his hand.

They were being watched.

Birch's warning was too late.

Strange mobs surrounded them.

"Piglins!" cried Emmy.

The piglins attacked Birch!
But they left Emmy alone.
They liked her gold helmet
and gold boots.

Emmy had an idea!
She took off her gold helmet
and put it on Birch's head.
The piglins stopped
fighting Birch.

20

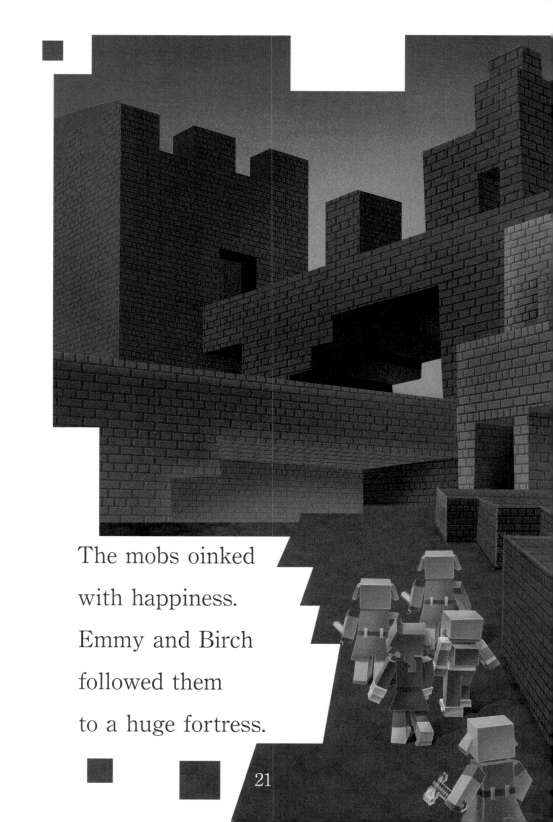

The mobs oinked
with happiness.
Emmy and Birch
followed them
to a huge fortress.

21

In the fortress,

they found a treasure room

filled with gold.

Birch opened a chest.

The piglins drew their swords

and made angry noises!

Emmy and Birch escaped
the mobs by smashing
a big hole in the wall.
On the other side was
a desert.

Piglins chased them.
It was very difficult to run.
"This is not ordinary sand,"
said Emmy.
"It is soul sand!"

Skeletons also started
firing arrows at them!
Emmy and Birch ran faster.
They could see a portal
on the other side of
a river of lava!

"We're trapped," said Birch.
Emmy pointed at two striders
with red skin and stringy hair.
"We can't cross the lava,"
said Emmy, "but striders can!"

Emmy saddled the striders.
She and Birch climbed onto
the passive mobs,
but the striders stood there,
chirping.

Emmy offered them carrots.
They just kept chirping.
Birch had an idea.
Carrots did not grow
in the Nether.
Maybe striders did not
eat them.

"Quick! Offer them the blue-green fungi," Birch shouted as a floating ghast joined the skeletons and piglins.

When the striders saw
the fungi,
they started running!
Emmy and Birch
raced toward
the portal.

On the other side of the portal,
they could see Byte.

He was waiting for them.

He had his stick in his mouth.

They were going to make it!

Safe in the Overworld,
Emmy threw the stick.
Byte fetched it,
and then Birch threw it.
Playing with Byte
was a great end
to a great adventure!